CUENTO DE LUZ

To my father.

To the children who live in conflict zones, so that they
can see their kite of PEACE flying high in the sky.

— Ana A. de Eulate

FUNDACIÓN COMETA

The author and illustrator will donate all proceeds
from this book to the Cometa Foundation.
www.fundacioncometa.org

The Sky of Afghanistan

Text © 2012 Ana A. de Eulate
Illustrations © 2012 Sonja Wimmer
This edition © 2012 Cuento de Luz SL
Calle Claveles 10 | Urb Monteclaro | Pozuelo de Alarcón | 28223 Madrid | Spain | www.cuentodeluz.com
Original title in Spanish: El cielo de Afganistán
English translation by Jon Brokenbrow

ISBN: 978-84-15503-04-0

Printed by Shanghai Chenxi Printing Co., Ltd. in PRC, April 2012, print number 1273-03

FSC
www.fsc.org
MIX
Paper from
responsible sources
FSC® C007923

The Sky
of Afghanistan

Ana A. de Eulate · Sonja Wimmer

I look at the sky, I close my eyes,
and my imagination begins to soar...

I fly between the clouds of the
country I love: Afghanistan.

The sky can be full of kites, I think to myself,
but it can also be full of dreams...

And mine flies up high, high into the sky,
towards the stars...

I'm a little Afghan girl,
who doesn't stop dreaming...
And my dream spreads
to all of the different regions,
entering people's houses,
their homes, their families,
their hearts...

It can be seen in the smiles of other children,
in their beautiful eyes, full of wonder
and the will to learn that my country has.
And in that smile, which despite being hidden,
is full of sweetness and serenity.

I want to fly high, high,
like a kite in the sky!
I want to feel the pull
of the string in my hand
as it struggles against the wind.

I feel that I can make this dream come true,
a wonderful dream in which we all hold hands,
and we are all given a new opportunity
to leave our footprints for all eternity.

In this eternity silence reigns,
and the sound of war has truly gone forever.

I will fly the bright kite of peace,
because it is possible, I am sure of it.

Because I am a little Afghan girl,
and I carry within me, within my heart,
all of the other names of innocent
people from my country.

And I carry within me a future
that will be built upon
foundations of hope.

I carry within me the certainty that everything is possible,
that enormous doors and windows can be opened
from which I can learn, from which I want to learn,

from where I can steer my kite
high into the sky, heading towards the stars,
towards the dawn.

And from where I will feel the wind
caressing my face,
where by closing my eyes
and opening my heart,
I will see my dream come true,
the same dream longed for
by all my people.

And then we will all walk together,
hand in hand, along the same path,
the path that leads us
to the place we have all longed for,
the place we have dreamed about
for so many years...

A place where harmony reigns,
a place of togetherness...
A place—please forgive me if my eyes fill with
tears—that leads us towards PEACE.